Frankenstein Doesn't Slam Hockey Pucks

**by Debbie Dadey
and
Marcia Thornton Jones**

illustrated by John Steven Gurney

A
LITTLE APPLE
PAPERBACK

SCHOLASTIC INC.
New York   Toronto   London   Auckland   Sydney
Mexico City   New Delhi   Hong Kong

*For the Kelkhoff's: Al, Barb, Doug,
and Kristin — DD*

*To Debbie Dadey, a great writer and an even better
friend! — MTJ*

ISBN 0-590-18984-0

Text copyright © 1998 by Marcia Thornton Jones and Debra S. Dadey.
Illustrations copyright © 1998 by Scholastic Inc.
All rights reserved. Published by Scholastic Inc.
LITTLE APPLE PAPERBACKS is a trademark of Scholastic Inc.
THE ADVENTURES OF THE BAILEY SCHOOL KIDS in design is a registered trademark of Scholastic Inc.

12 11 10 9 8 7 6 5 4 3 2 1   9/9 0 1 2 3/0

Printed in the U.S.A.   40

First Scholastic printing, January 1999

Contents

1

Dizzy

"Quit that," Eddie told his friend Liza. Liza twirled around one more time and looked at her friends Eddie, Melody, and Howie. "I'm just practicing for my figure skating class. I have a lesson today."

"I always knew you were dizzy," Eddie said, "but now you're making me dizzy, too."

"It's fun," Liza said. "You should try it." The four kids stood in their favorite after-school meeting place, under the big oak tree on the playground. Liza twirled around one more time and made her blond ponytail swirl in the crisp spring breeze.

"Stop," Eddie said, "before I throw up."

Liza stopped and picked up her blue

Bailey School backpack. "Okay, I'll stop. I have to go to skating practice anyway."

"I thought the ice rink was closed for remodeling," Howie said.

Liza shook her head. "It reopened this week. You should come with me. I've heard the new owners made the rink really nice."

"Why don't we all go watch Liza practice?" Melody asked.

"Sounds good to me," Howie said.

Eddie groaned. "I don't want to watch prissy skaters twirl around on the ice. I want to play soccer."

"Then you'll have to play by yourself, because we're going with Liza." Melody grabbed her book bag and walked off with Liza and Howie. A thin layer of snow covered the ground and with every footstep Melody made a crunching sound.

Eddie shoved his red curly hair under his Bailey School ball cap. "All right," he muttered. "I'll come, but I'll probably be bored into little ice cubes."

As they kicked through the snow, another third-grader made her way across the playground. Carey hurried to catch up with the four friends. "Are you going to the new skating rink?" she asked Eddie in her sweetest voice. Carey's father was the president of the Bailey City Bank and she usually got whatever she wanted. Everybody at Bailey Elementary knew she liked Eddie. "I'm going to the rink, too. I'll let you carry my books for

me," Carey added, holding out her book bag.

"And I'll let you be kidnapped by aliens," Eddie muttered as he shoved past her.

Carey hurried after the four friends as they walked down Forest Lane toward the rink.

"It's a good thing they remodeled that place," Howie said. "It was about to cave in."

Carey nodded. "The old owners, Mr. and Mrs. England, just didn't have the money to fix it up so they sold it to the F. N. Stein Corporation."

"I feel sorry for Mr. and Mrs. England," Liza said. "They're pretty old, and I think they will miss the rink."

"What's to miss?" Eddie said. "They'll probably lie on the beach in Florida for the rest of their lives."

"That sounds good to me," Melody said. She shivered as a cold breeze made her pull her jacket hood over her dark hair.

"Going to the beach in the winter is great," Carey interrupted. "I know because my daddy is taking me on a cruise to a tropical island. We're leaving Monday. I get to miss an entire week of school, too."

"As far as I'm concerned," Eddie said, "you can get stranded on that island for the rest of my life."

"Stop fighting," Liza said. "We're almost there."

The five kids rounded the corner and stopped in front of the ice rink to stare. Howie was the first to speak. "Oh, my gosh," he gulped. "What have they done?"

2

Hockey Puck

"Holy Toledo!" Eddie hollered. "This is great!"

"It sure is fancy," Melody agreed. The kids stared at the orange neon sign for the Bailey City Ice Skating Complex. Orange bolts of lightning covered the entire front of the bright white building.

"Come on," Liza said, "I can't wait to see the inside."

Bright purple signs hung over a snack bar complete with purple tables and chairs. A big room off to the side held dozens of flashing video games.

"Cool," Eddie said. "I could spend every afternoon in here."

"If you had any money," Melody reminded him.

"Let's look in here," Liza suggested.

She led them through two bright green swinging doors into a room that overlooked the rinks. In the center of the room stood a huge green metal fireplace. It was round with a bench circling it, but there was no fire.

"Brrr," Eddie complained. "It's cold in here. Doesn't that fireplace work?"

Carey pointed to the huge glass windows that looked out onto big ice rinks. "It has to be cold for the ice to freeze."

"This looks cool," Melody said, pointing to a brightly colored poster on the wall. The poster read JOIN THE JUNIOR THUNDERBOLTS HOCKEY TEAM. SIGN UP IN THE OFFICE. An arrow pointed up some steps.

"All right," Eddie cheered. "They're starting a kids' team."

"Hockey is neat," Melody admitted. "My dad took me to a game in Sheldon City one time."

"Let's sign up," Howie said.

Liza's face turned as white as the ice.

"No way," she said. "Hockey is too rough. I could get hurt."

"You could get hurt looking in the mirror," Eddie teased.

"I bet hockey would be fun," Howie told Liza and Carey. "Besides, you both already know how to skate."

"No thanks," Carey said, shaking her head firmly. "I'm staying in my figure skating class."

"I'll stick with figure skating, too," Liza agreed. "Nobody tries to hit you."

"Not usually," Melody admitted, "but I still think it would be fun to try hockey."

"You're crazy," Carey said, walking away. "I'm going to get my skates on."

"Let's sign up," Eddie said. "I'd rather slam a hockey puck around than just skate in circles."

"After all," Howie said, "what's the worst thing that could happen?"

"Nothing except a lot of fun," Melody said.

a shelf stretched from one corner to the next. On the shelf was a row of beakers, bottles, and test tubes. But they were not the most unusual things in the room. A huge wooden chair with a metal cap filled the center of the room. It was big enough for all four kids to sit on at once. Directly over the chair was a small skylight.

Eddie headed toward the chair, but a deep voice from the doorway stopped him dead in his tracks.

3

Hrrrmm

"Hrrrmm?" the stranger said.

Liza, Melody, Howie, and Eddie turned and looked up. The man's shoulders were so wide, he had to turn sideways to get through the door. He had to duck so his head wouldn't bump the door frame. The man wore an old slime-green Bailey City Thunderbolts hockey jersey. His skin was pale except for a huge purple scar stretching across his cheek.

"Oh, my gosh," Liza squealed. "We know you."

The four kids gulped when they remembered the huge man from a school field trip to the Shelley Museum of Science. He was Frank, the museum assistant.

"It's nice to see you again," Melody

said nervously. "What are you doing here?"

"Hrrrmm," Frank grunted. "I work here now."

Liza's face grew pale, but Eddie didn't pay any attention. "We want to sign up for the hockey team," he said.

Frank strode across the office to grab some papers. The floor shook with every step he took. He handed a paper to each of the four kids. "Parents must sign permission slip before joining my winning team."

"How do you know the new team will be lucky enough to win?" Melody asked.

Frank picked up a test tube and grunted. "I have a good feeling."

"I have a bad feeling," Liza said, grabbing Melody's arm and pulling her toward the door. "Let's go."

"What's wrong with you?" Eddie said after Liza hurried back into the main lobby.

"What's wrong?" Liza squealed. "What

do you mean? Don't you know who that was back there?"

"You mean Frank? Lots of people change jobs. Now he's the hockey coach," Eddie said. "I can't wait to start playing."

"You can't be serious," Liza said.

Eddie grinned. "I'm as serious as a heart attack. Of course I want to play."

Liza put her hand on Eddie's sleeve. "Listen to me," Liza said. "You can't play hockey with Frank as a coach."

Eddie rolled his eyes. "I could play hockey with a porcupine for a coach if I wanted to. What's wrong with you, any-way?"

Liza pointed a finger right at Eddie's nose. "There's a hockey-playing monster in this ice rink."

Melody giggled. "And his name is Eddie."

Howie shook his head. "I don't think Liza is talking about Eddie. I think she's talking about Frank."

"That's right," Liza said. "Don't you remember anything?"

"I remember that it's time to play soccer," Eddie said.

"And I remember it's time for your ice-skating lesson," Melody said.

"It is, but that's not the problem," Liza said. "The problem is that Frank is the one and only Frankenstein monster."

4

Monster Team

"We never proved that Frank was a monster," Eddie told Liza. The four friends had hurried away from Frank's office and were huddled around the cold fireplace.

"Maybe not, but don't you remember the secret laboratory?" Liza said. Her three friends thought about the mysterious room they had found on their field trip to the museum. It was filled with strange science equipment belonging to Frank's boss, Dr. Victor. That wasn't all. There was also a locked refrigerator that was perfect for storing monster parts.

Melody finally shrugged. "Lots of scientists have laboratories," she said.

"Eddie is right. We never proved a thing," Howie said.

Liza grabbed Melody's arm. "But you must remember Frank's petunias."

Melody smiled. "Of course. They were beautiful."

Howie nodded. "His flowers were the biggest flowers I've ever seen."

"Exactly!" Liza gasped. "You're starting to understand."

"I understand," Eddie said with a laugh, "that you are the biggest nut on ice!"

"I'm not," Liza said seriously. "Frank is a monster on ice. I have a feeling your monster hockey coach is planning a *big* surprise. We have to stop him before it's too late."

"We are too late," Eddie said. "Your brains turned into monster slush the minute we walked into this skating rink!"

"My brains are fine," Liza told him. "But I remember something that may threaten every hockey player in Bailey City."

"What?" Eddie asked. "Are you planning to give them one of your school pictures?"

"No," Liza said. "I think Frank is planning on turning an ordinary hockey team into monsters just like him."

"How can a coach turn normal players like me into monsters?" Eddie asked.

"You're not normal," Melody said.

Howie laughed. "And teachers already think you are a monster!"

Eddie curled his fist and held it in front of him. "I'm about to give all of you a monster-sized knuckle sandwich," he said.

"Fight all you want," Liza said. "But when you come face-to-face with a team filled with Frankenstein monsters, that little fist of yours won't even be enough to give them a bruise."

Melody patted Liza on the shoulder. "I think you're getting upset over nothing," she told her friend. "It would take magic to do what you're talking about."

"Magic," Liza said slowly, "or a stolen secret formula."

Howie's eyes got big. "I know what Liza is talking about," he said. "Right before we left the museum Dr. Victor found a bottle Frank had hidden. It was labeled FORMULA BIG."

"That's right!" Melody said. "Dr. Victor was very upset with Frank for taking it from his secret laboratory."

"And I'm very upset with all of you," Eddie said. "I've had enough talk about science experiments and secret formulas. I know a formula for fun. It's called hockey."

"You can't be serious about signing up for Frank's team," Liza said.

"I'll show you how serious I am," Eddie told her. "I'm going to get my grandmother to sign this permission slip right now." Eddie hurried from the rink before Liza could utter another word.

5

Monster Lesson

Eddie pushed Howie and Melody down the sidewalk the next afternoon.

"Hurry," he said. "I don't want to be late for our first day of hockey practice."

Liza had to run to keep up with them. "You can't play hockey with Frankenstein. Besides, you don't even know how to skate," she said. She pretended to zoom across the ice and turned in circles until she was dizzy.

"Hockey is not about skating, ice brains," Eddie told her. "It's about slamming hockey pucks to the edge of the earth and back."

"You can't do that," Melody reminded him, "if you keep falling down."

"The girls have a point," Howie said. "We're going to have to become better skaters before we can beat the pants off another hockey team."

"I'll show you what it takes to be champs," Eddie argued, "as soon as we get to the rink."

When the kids went inside the rink, they dumped their book bags on the benches and hurried to join the rest of the Junior Thunderbolts hockey team. Liza sat down in the bleachers to watch.

Frank was explaining the safety rules of the game. When he held up the plain blue helmet the kids had to wear, Eddie let out a groan.

"That's just an ordinary helmet," Eddie complained. "A team called the Thunderbolts ought to wear something flashy."

Frank locked his eyes on Eddie. "Hrrrmm?" Frank asked.

Eddie grinned. "How about some lightning bolts on the side of the helmet?"

"Hrrrmm." Frank nodded. "Lightning is good."

"How about glittery flames on the shirt?" Melody suggested.

Frank dropped the helmet on the ice and bellowed, "Hrrrmmm! Fire bad!"

"Melody," Howie whispered. "Don't you remember? Frank is afraid of fire."

Melody gulped. "Sorry. How about nice lightning bolts on the shirt, too?" she suggested.

"Good," Frank grunted. "Now we play hockey."

"All right!" Eddie yelled. "Let's do it. We'll be the best team."

Frank nodded and the purple scar on his face wiggled. "That is why we will start our practice with ice-skating."

"SKATING!" Eddie blurted. "That's for sissies wearing tutus."

Frank grunted at Eddie. "Hrrrmm. Are you calling me a sissy?" Frank asked.

"Uhmm . . ." Eddie muttered as he backed away from the giant hockey coach, "of course not. It's just that I thought we'd be hitting hockey pucks."

Frank nodded. "Before hitting pucks, you must skate. Follow me."

Frank glided onto the ice and the rest of the team tried to follow. They hadn't gone far before most of them stumbled and fell. Everyone soon realized they wouldn't have a winning team unless they could keep from falling. Once they had practiced skating around the rink, Frank gathered them in the center of the ice.

"Must follow puck," Frank said, "even when hit behind you."

"But we'd have to skate backward," Howie blurted. "It's hard enough going forward."

Frank nodded. "You must skate in all directions."

"No way," Melody said. "I'm barely able to skate in a straight line."

"I will teach you," Frank said. "Grab on." Frank held out his hockey stick. Melody, Howie, and Eddie grabbed it. Frank pushed them around the rink as if they were feathers. As Frank skated, the kids figured out what to do with their skates. After they had circled the ice three times, Frank pushed other kids around the rink.

"Tomorrow," he said after giving every kid a chance to practice, "you will be even better." Then Frank left the kids and sped across the ice.

"Wow," Howie said when Liza hurried

a giant iceberg. That can mean only one thing. Frankenstein loves the ice."

"Just like Frank," Liza said. "I bet the North Pole is where Frank learned to ice-skate."

Howie nodded. "Maybe he got all his scars in the North Pole, playing hockey."

Eddie shook his head and laughed. "No, the North Pole is busy with Santa and his elves. I'm pretty sure there's no room for Frankenstein."

Melody giggled. "Maybe Eddie's right," she said. "After all, it seems pretty weird to think about a monster playing hockey."

"Yeah," Eddie said. "I'm sure Frankenstein doesn't slam hockey pucks."

"How do you know so much about Frankenstein?" Liza asked Howie.

"I watched a program on the History Channel about him last week," Howie explained.

Eddie sat down on a bench to pull off his skates. "Hey, I watched part of that."

Liza, Melody, and Howie looked at Eddie in surprise. "You watched the History Channel?" Melody asked. Eddie was not known for doing anything educational unless he had to.

Eddie shrugged. "My grandmother made me. She said I might as well learn something if I wanted to watch TV."

"Did you learn anything?" Liza giggled as her other two friends sat down to untie their skates.

Eddie scratched his red hair and tried to remember. "I remember that all Frankenstein wanted was to have a friend."

"That's so sad," Liza said.

Eddie continued talking. "But no one liked him and he ended up killing everybody."

Liza's eyes got big and she gulped. "Oh, my gosh. Is that the reason Frank came back to Bailey City?"

7

Formula Big

"Liza," Eddie said, putting his hand on Liza's shoulder. "I think you've been studying too hard lately. You've gone a little cuckoo."

Melody nodded. "Frank came to Bailey City to play hockey, nothing else."

"I think Frank came to get away from Dr. Victor, the museum director," Liza said softly, looking around to make sure Frank wasn't nearby. Frank was at the other end of the ice rink talking to fourth-graders.

"Why would Frank run away from Dr. Victor?" Howie asked. "If Frank wanted to leave the science museum all he had to do was quit his job."

"Not if they had a fight," Liza said,

36

shaking her head. "Or if Frank stole something valuable from Dr. Victor."

Eddie wiped off his skates and threw the ice at Liza. "You shouldn't say bad stuff about people. You're always telling me that."

"I know," Liza admitted. "But I have a reason. When we were in Frank's office I saw a bottle marked FORMULA BIG."

"Oh, my gosh," Melody said. "That's Dr. Victor's secret formula from the Shelley Museum."

"What would Frank be doing with it?" Howie asked. "Unless he wants to grow big flowers like he had at the museum."

"I bet he plans to create a monster hockey team so he can have friends," Liza said seriously.

"Cool," Eddie said. "Maybe I better go get some of that stuff."

"Don't even think about it," Melody said. "You don't know what that could do to you. It might make your eyeballs pop out."

"Gross," Liza squealed.

"This is just a bunch of baloney," Eddie said. "I'm sure Dr. Victor knows exactly where Frank is and everything is just hunky-dory."

"I know one way to find out," Melody said. "I'll ask Frank. He's coming this way." Melody walked over to the edge of the rink. She waited until Frank skated beside them, then she reached out and patted him on the arm.

"Hrrrmm?" Frank asked.

"Excuse me," Melody said. "But we remember you from the Shelley Museum and we were just wondering where Dr. Victor is."

Frank growled, "HRRRMM! Dr. Victor mad!" He took his hockey stick and hit a puck so hard it shattered the nearby boards. Then Frank skated away from Melody as fast as he could.

"That proves it," Liza said. "Frank is mad at Dr. Victor."

Howie sat down and pulled off his skates. "I don't think that proves anything."

"There is one way to prove it for sure," Liza said slowly, "but it would be dangerous. Very dangerous."

8

Winning Formula

The next afternoon Howie, Melody, and Eddie met at the skating rink. Liza was already in the middle of her skating lesson, spinning in tiny circles.

"Liza is getting to be a good skater," Melody pointed out. "She looks fantastic."

"Carey doesn't look very good at all," Eddie said with a laugh. "She reminds me of stomach medicine."

Carey wore a fluffy hat and scarf, tights, and a skating skirt. All of it was bright pink. Liza skated beside her in black pants and a gray sweater. Eddie stuck out his tongue at Carey.

"Wow!" Howie yelled. "Did you see Liza make a figure eight? I didn't know she was that good."

"It looks sissy to me," Eddie said, zipping up his coat to stay warm.

Carey and Liza skated up to where Eddie, Melody, and Howie stood. "Hello," Carey said, batting her eyelashes at Eddie. "How are you?"

Eddie barely looked at Carey and answered, "I'm cold."

"It's almost spring," Carey said, "but I'm cold, too. That's why I'm glad I'm going to a tropical island this weekend," she bragged. "It's so warm there."

"I'll be glad when she's anywhere but here," Eddie said when Carey skated away.

"We'd better hurry," Melody said. "Frank is starting hockey practice."

Frank was already skating on the other ice rink. He had a hockey stick and was slamming pucks into the goal.

"Cool," Eddie said. "Let's get our skates."

The kids hurried to put on their skates, but Liza stopped them before they got on the ice. She was finished with her lesson and looked worried. "What's wrong now?" Eddie asked.

"Are you sure you want to skate near a monster with a hockey stick?" she asked. "It could be very dangerous."

"Your mind is dangerous," Eddie said. He thumbed his nose at Liza and got on the ice. He skated toward Frank. Howie and Melody followed. "We're ready for hockey practice," Eddie told Frank.

"Hrrrmm," Frank said with a nod, "and I am ready for you." Frank skated over to a closet at the end of the rink.

"All right," Eddie said. "We're finally getting hockey sticks."

Howie shook his head. "It looks more like we're going to be cleaning the floor."

Frank handed each kid a broom instead of a hockey stick. "We use brooms to learn sweeping the puck," Frank said.

Eddie frowned. "I didn't come here to do girly housework," he complained.

Melody pointed her broom at Eddie. "You'd better take that back or I'll have to knock you to the North Pole."

Eddie whacked Melody's broom with his own.

"Oh, no," Howie said. "There's a fight."

Frank skated between Eddie and Melody. Without a word he lifted them both off the ice. "Fighting wrong," Frank said. "Be nice. Fighting loses friends."

"I thought fighting was part of hockey," Howie said as Eddie and Melody dangled from Frank's arms.

"Teams working together make winning formula." Frank set Melody and Eddie down before skating over to give other kids their brooms. Liza leaned over the railing to listen to her friends.

"Did you hear that?" Howie said. "He was talking about a formula. Maybe Liza is right."

"Frank is only talking about what it takes to win," Eddie argued. "Hockey

teams are supposed to beat other hockey teams."

"There is a way to prove Frank is Frankenstein's monster," Liza said, "but it is too dangerous."

"That's what you said yesterday," Melody told her. "You never told us your plan."

Liza didn't get to explain because Frank glided over to them. He stopped suddenly. His skates sprayed the kids with ice. "Hockey means control," Frank said.

"That doesn't explain why I need this broom," Eddie said. "If I wanted to do housework, I would've stayed home with my grandmother."

Frank laughed. "Hrrrmm. No cleaning," he said. "We will sweep our way to winning."

"You're kidding, right?" Eddie asked. "Everybody knows hockey is all about slamming the puck down the throats of the enemy."

Frank glared at Eddie and bent down until his nose nearly touched Eddie's. The purple scar on Frank's cheek throbbed. Eddie backed away, but Frank came closer and closer.

9

Slap Shot

Frank stared straight into Eddie's eyes. "Hrrrmm," Frank growled. "I never lie."

Eddie tried to take another step back, but his skates got tangled in the broom and he sat down hard on the ice. The rest of the Junior Thunderbolts laughed and Eddie's face turned as red as his hair. Frank skated off to help another group of hockey players.

"I'll show him," Eddie muttered. "Nobody makes a fool out of me."

"You better not mess with Frank," Howie warned. "Monsters can be very fierce."

"Not as fierce as me," Eddie said. "Just wait."

Frank showed the team how to use the brooms to carry the puck with gentle sweeping motions. Liza watched from the nearby bleachers. When Frank lined up all the kids at one end of the rink, Eddie went into action.

"AAAAGGGGGHHHH!" Eddie let out a bloodcurdling battle cry to get everybody's attention. "Watch me beat the earmuffs off every one of you!"

Eddie raised his broom high in the air. Then he brought it down and slammed his hockey puck with a mighty slap shot. He staggered back from the force of his swing, but he didn't fall down. He was determined to see that puck go into the goal.

It didn't. The puck hit the wall and bounced back quickly in Eddie's direction. The little black puck sped right toward Eddie. He tried to dodge the puck, and, as he did, he lost his balance. Eddie landed with a thud right in front of the entire team.

"It looks like Eddie got swept up,"

Melody said with a giggle just as Frank skidded to a stop in front of the kids.

Frank glared down at Eddie. "Hrrrmmm. Mad is bad," Frank warned Eddie. "To win, always be in control."

Eddie gulped and nodded. But as soon as Frank skated away, Eddie slammed his broom on the ice.

Liza leaned over the railing and giggled. "You better practice skating or you're going to be in trouble."

Howie held out a hand and helped Eddie up. "If Frank is a monster," Howie said slowly, "I have a feeling we may all be in trouble."

"Don't tell me you believe Liza is right," Eddie begged.

"I am right," Liza said. "Follow me. I'm going to close the book on this Frankenstein story once and for all."

10

Frank's Super Formula

Liza checked to make sure Frank wasn't watching and motioned for her friends to follow. They pulled off their skates and crept after Liza all the way to Frank's office.

"We shouldn't be here," Liza warned. "This office is private property, but it's the only way to prove Frank is a monster."

Howie nodded. "Let's do it," he said as he grabbed the doorknob.

The four kids sneaked into Frank's office and closed the door. The huge wooden chair cast dark shadows across the dimly lit room. "Now that we're here, how are you going to prove anything?" Eddie asked.

"A cold-blooded monster wouldn't

have hockey notes piled on his desk," Melody said. "All we have to do is look there and you will see that Frank is only a hockey coach and nothing more."

"Just make sure you stay away from that chair," Liza warned.

"Why?" Eddie asked. "It's so big we could all sit in it and be comfortable."

"Don't even think of it," Liza said. "A chair like that could be good for only one thing. Attracting lightning." Liza pointed to the window right over the chair. "I bet that's where Frank sits to get juiced up. The lightning comes right through that window and into his chair."

"Well, we could all use a little more energy," Melody said with a grin.

"Not that kind of energy," Howie said. "Liza's right. Until we're sure, stay away from that chair."

Howie, Melody, and Eddie hurried to Frank's desk. It was piled with papers. The three friends dug through the papers.

Liza didn't follow her friends. Instead, she made her way to the side of the room and examined the shelf full of beakers, test tubes, and bottles. She carefully read each label. When she got to the last bottle she gasped. "This is even worse than I thought!" Liza said.

Melody, Howie, and Eddie stopped shuffling through the papers on Frank's desk and hurried to where Liza stood.

"What is it?' Melody asked.

Liza pointed to the tall green bottle sitting on the shelf. A yellow label with scribbly writing said FRANK'S SUPER-SPECIAL HOCKEY FORMULA B. "That can only mean one thing," Liza said. "Frank really is trying to make a monster hockey team."

"It doesn't mean ice cubes," Howie said. "It could be an athlete protein shake."

"I know how to find out," Eddie said as he reached for the bottle.

Melody grabbed Eddie's arm. "You better not touch that bottle," she warned. "There is no telling what's in it."

"I know what it is," Liza said softly. "It's the formula Dr. Victor created to help Frank grow into a monster. Only Frank has added something to it."

"You can't be sure of that," Howie said, but his voice shook when he spoke. "After all, how would Frank know how to concoct a magic formula that makes people grow?"

"Not people," Liza said. "Monsters. Frank knows exactly how to mix formulas. After all, he was an assistant to a mad scientist for years."

Melody opened her mouth to argue. But a loud voice in the hallway stopped her before she spoke. It was Frank and he was right outside the door.

"Frank is coming," Liza gasped.

"There's only one thing to do," Eddie said bravely. "We have to fight."

"Or hide," Howie suggested.

"Where can we hide?" Melody whispered.

Howie pointed behind the huge wooden chair.

"No way," Liza whined. "I'm not getting near that lightning magnet."

"It's either that," Howie said simply, "or face an angry monster."

"Howie's right," Eddie said as he scrambled behind the chair. "Hurry, before Frank gets here."

The four kids squeezed behind the giant wooden chair just as Frank threw open the door and marched to his desk. Another giant man followed him into the room before slamming the door.

"Our team," Frank said with a laugh from deep inside his chest, "will be winners, just like the Junior Thunderbolts will be."

"Our team has not been together long," the man told Frank. "We may not be as strong as the other team. We could lose."

Frank thumped his fist on the side of

the chair. "We practiced. We worked hard. And," Frank added, his voice dropping to a whisper, "our team has my secret formula."

"The rest of the team isn't as sure as you," the man argued. "They do not believe your formula for winning will work."

"HHHRRRMMM!" bellowed Frank. "They must believe. We grow bigger and stronger each day. We *will* win Saturday. We will conquer all."

11

The Plan

"What are we going to do?" Liza said.

"What are you talking about?" Eddie asked. Eddie, Liza, Melody, and Howie were under the big oak tree on the school playground. It was Friday afternoon, two days after they had hidden in Frank's office.

Liza stamped her foot. "We have to think of a way to stop this monster hockey team invasion."

"Why don't you stomp them to death?" Eddie snickered.

"Maybe we could call the police," Melody suggested.

"I thought you didn't believe Frank was really the Frankenstein monster," Howie asked Melody.

"I don't," Melody said slowly, "but it

wouldn't hurt to call the police just to be sure."

Eddie pulled off his baseball cap and looked at Melody. "What would we tell the police? Oh, by the way, our hockey coach is a zillion-year-old Frankenstein monster. He's back from the dead to take over our city."

"Eddie's right," Howie agreed. "They would think we're crazy. It's up to us to save Bailey City."

"I know what we can do," Eddie said suddenly.

"What?" Liza asked hopefully.

Eddie laughed. "I'll go home and get my monster exterminator gun. I'll zap all the monsters over the rainbow."

"This is serious," Howie told Eddie. "We've got to think of a plan."

The four kids sat together under the oak tree. Then they stood up and leaned against the tree. "It's no good," Melody said. "I can't think of anything."

"Me neither," Liza moaned. "We're

doomed to become little Frankenstein monsters."

"What's wrong with you guys?" Carey said. She was dressed in a fancy blue skating skirt and matching jacket. A pair of white ice skates hung over her shoulder.

"We're scared that monsters are going to take over our city," Liza blurted out.

"Shh," Melody said.

"Ha-ha," Carey laughed and pushed her blond curls out of her face. "You guys are so funny. Brrr, aren't you cold? I'll be glad to be someplace warm. Tomorrow I leave on my cruise to a warm sunny island. I can't wait."

"We can't wait, either," Eddie muttered. "Why don't you leave now?"

Carey stuck her nose up in the air. "I was trying to be nice and you're just mean, mean, and more mean," she said with a sniff. "I'll think of you when I'm on the biggest cruise ship in the world having the time of my life."

"You shouldn't fight with Carey," Liza warned Eddie as soon as Carey stomped away. "It isn't nice."

"Liza is right," Howie said. "Remember what Frank said."

Melody nodded. "He said mad is bad. We should all work together."

"That's in hockey," Eddie said. "Carey is worse than a Frankenstein monster so she doesn't count."

"Everybody counts," Howie said.

Liza jumped up and down. "Whoop-te-do!" Liza yelled. "You just saved Bailey City! Follow me!" Liza raced down the sidewalk. Melody, Eddie, and Howie looked at one another and shrugged. Then they ran after Liza.

Liza didn't stop running until she got to a pay phone in front of Burger Doodle. She had already found the number in a phone book and was dialing by the time her friends caught up.

"This is no time to call dial-a-date," Eddie told her.

"I'm not calling a date," Liza said. "I'm calling the one person that can save us from monster madness. Dr. Victor!"

"Are you crazy?" Melody asked. "The last person you should call is a mad scientist."

But it was too late. Dr. Victor answered the phone and Liza started talking.

12

Eddie's Great Assist

Eddie folded his arms over his chest and stomped his right foot. "I'm not doing it," he said, "and that's final."

Liza had just hung up the phone and told her friends the plan. Eddie did not look happy.

"It's our only idea for saving Bailey City from a monster takeover," Liza said.

"You don't know your plan will work," Eddie argued. "You can't even prove Frank is a monster."

"That's true," Howie said, "but it won't hurt to try."

"Yes it will," Eddie said. "It will be agonizing torture."

"I've already called Dr. Victor," Liza said. "Time is running out."

"Say you'll do it," Melody urged. "Please?"

Before Eddie could make up his mind, a long black van with dark windows sped past the corner where the four kids argued. SHELLEY MUSEUM OF SCIENCE was painted on the side in bold yellow letters.

Howie put his hand on Eddie's shoulder. "It's now or never," he said. "Bailey City is counting on you."

Eddie took a deep breath and nodded. "I'll do it," he said. "But I'm not going to like it!"

"Thank you, Eddie," Melody said. "We all know how hard this is for you."

"We'd better hurry," Liza said. "It will be a disaster if Dr. Victor gets to the skating rink before us."

The four friends raced to the skating rink. They barely made it in time. Dr. Victor was just climbing out of his van when the kids hurried into the rink.

Carey was skating figure eights in the

middle of the rink. At the far side, Frank and the Junior Thunderbolts' goaltender practiced wrist shots. Liza, Melody, and Howie quickly laced on their skates and sped onto the ice. Eddie wobbled behind them just as Dr. Victor entered the rink.

Dr. Victor glared at Frank as soon as he saw him. Dr. Victor looked so mad that even his bald head turned a bright red. "You cannot hide in this skating rink behind your hockey pads," he yelled to Frank and stepped to the edge of the ice.

"How did you find me here?" Frank growled.

Dr. Victor smiled. "A phone call from an unknown friend," he yelled to Frank. "What matters is that I am here. You cannot win against me!"

"HHHRRRRMMMM!" Frank roared and threw his hockey stick across the ice. Then he started skating straight toward Dr. Victor.

"That's a hockey violation," Howie

mumbled so only his friends could hear. "If we were playing a game Frank would end up in the penalty box."

"The face-off has started," Melody said. "We have more to worry about than breaking hockey rules."

Liza gave Eddie a little shove toward Carey. "It's time for your power play," Liza told him. "Go make the assist."

Eddie gulped, but then he pushed off with his skate just as Carey zipped by. "Carey, wait," he hollered so everyone in the rink would hear. "I have to tell you something."

13

Bailey City Monster

Carey did a fancy turn and stopped to face Eddie. She folded her arms in front of her stomach and frowned. "I thought you wanted to get rid of me."

Eddie's face turned red. "Me? I was just joking."

Melody, Liza, and Howie scooted to the middle of the rink to stand next to Eddie. Together, the five kids blocked Frank's way. Frank tried to go around but Eddie's words stopped Frank cold.

"I wanted to tell you," Eddie said loudly, "I'm . . . er . . . I'm SORRY!"

Carey gasped. Then she wobbled and fell flat on her bottom. "WHAT DID YOU SAY?" she asked.

Eddie's face turned sickly green, but

he spoke up anyway. "I made you mad, so I want to apologize."

"You've never apologized in your life!" Carey told Eddie.

Melody nodded. "He knows better now," she said.

"Thanks to Frank," Howie said.

Frank frowned. "Hhhrrrmmm?" he asked.

"That's right," Eddie told Frank. "You said fighting loses friends."

"And that working together makes a winning formula," Liza added.

Frank looked at the kids. Then he looked at Dr. Victor. "Friends?" Frank said.

Dr. Victor smiled. "The kids are right," Dr. Victor said. "I still want to be your friend."

Frank looked confused. "But . . . you were mad."

"Friends get mad sometimes," Melody told Frank. "We're mad at Eddie all the time."

"But that doesn't mean we can't be friends anymore," Howie said.

"It just means we have to work things out," Liza said.

"If that is what you told your Junior Thunderbolts," Dr. Victor said with a smile, "then you have created a super-duper winning formula!"

"So what's it going to be?" Eddie asked Frank. "Are you still friends with Dr. Victor?"

Frank looked at Eddie. He looked at Carey sitting on the ice. Then he looked at Dr. Victor and smiled. "Friends," Frank said and he skated over to Dr. Victor to shake hands.

"Whew," Howie said. "That was a close call."

"But thanks to Liza we have nothing to worry about," Melody said. "Her plan changed a mad monster into a friendly giant."

"No," Liza said. "Thank Eddie."

Carey held out her hand and batted

her eyelashes at Eddie. "I will thank Eddie as soon as he helps me up," she said in a sweet voice.

"Don't thank me," Eddie said, "because I'm not going to help you do anything."

"But you said you were sorry," Carey blurted. "Were you just making that up?"

Eddie shook his head and grinned. "I am sorry. I'm sorry I have to hear all about your cruise. I'm sorry you go to Bailey School. I'm sorry you can't move to the North Pole and float on icebergs. I'm sorry, sorry, SORRY!"

"Oh no," Liza moaned. "We just saved Bailey City from a mad monster, but now we've created another one."

"You're right," Melody said. "This monster could be even worse!"

"And his name," Howie said with a giggle, "is Eddie!"